For Eliza, Anna and Kate

First published 2009 by Walker Books Ltd, 87 Vauxhall Walk, London SE11 5HJ

This edition published 2011

2 4 6 8 10 9 7 5 3

© 2009 Emma Chichester Clark

The right of Emma Chichester Clark to be identified as author/illustrator of this work has been
asserted by her in accordance with the Copyright, Designs and Patents Act 1988

This book has been typeset in Rialto DF Printed in China

British Library Cataloguing in Publication Data: a catalogue record for this book
is available from the British Library

ISBN 978-1-4063-3075-5

www.walker.co.uk

Goldilocks
and the Three Bears

EMMA CHICHESTER CLARK

WALKER BOOKS
AND SUBSIDIARIES
LONDON • BOSTON • SYDNEY • AUCKLAND

Once upon a time, there was a family of bears:
Mummy Bear, Daddy Bear and Baby Bear.
One morning, Mummy Bear said
"*Bother!* This porridge is much too hot!"

"Never mind, darling,"
said Daddy Bear.
"Let's go for a stroll
while it cools."
But that day, as they
were leaving, a little girl
called Goldilocks came
by, and goodness, was
she hungry!

Goldilocks walked straight into the bears' kitchen. "Mmmm! That porridge smells good," she said.

She didn't wonder. She didn't ask.

She stuck a spoon into the biggest bowl and swallowed an enormous mouthful. "Eeuch!" she cried. "Disgusting and *cold!*"

Then she dipped a spoon
in the middle-sized bowl.
"Whoaaar! Eeek! Boiling *hot!*"

Last of all she plunged
a spoon into the
littlest bowl.
"Mmm!" she sighed.
"Yummy!" she cried.
"This is *my* kind
of porridge!"
It was exactly right, so
she ate the whole lot.

After a nose through
the shelves, Goldilocks
found something to read.
"Now I need somewhere
to sit," she said.

She didn't wonder.
She didn't ask.
She plonked herself down
on the biggest chair.

"Yeeow!" she cried.
"What a dreadful *hard* chair!"

She tried to get comfy in the middle-sized chair.

"Oh! Too *soft*! Awful!" she groaned, as she sank into the cushions.

At last she spotted the smallest chair. "Aaah," she sighed. "Bravo!" she cried. "That is *my* kind of chair!"

But...
snap!
crack!
It broke into pieces.
"Stupid thing!" said
Goldilocks, shaking
out her hair.

"I s'pose," she thought,
"there'll be beds upstairs."

She didn't wonder.
She didn't ask.

She climbed up onto
the biggest bed.
"Beastly!" cried
Goldilocks.
"It's much too hard!"

She leapt on
the second, the
middle-sized bed.
"Oh save me!"
she screamed.
"It's so stiflingly
smotheringly,
suffocatingly,
soft!"

"There's got to be something
that's just right for me!"
she grumbled.

And what did
she see…?

"Oooh!" she sighed.
"Bullseye!" she cried.
"Now that's *my*
kind of bed!"

It wasn't too hard
and it wasn't too soft.
It was as right as right
could be. Goldilocks
climbed in.

Meanwhile, our friends the family
of bears, had arrived back home.
"I'm hungry!"
said Daddy Bear.
"I'm starving!"
said Mummy Bear.
"And I'm absolutely ravenous!"
said Baby Bear.

But... "HEY!"
roared Daddy Bear.
"Someone's been eating
my porridge!"

"Oh *my!*" gasped Mummy Bear. "*Someone's* been eating *my* porridge!"

"Where's mine?" squealed Baby Bear.

"Someone's been eating my porridge *and they've eaten it all up!*" cried Baby Bear.

"Oh, my poor darling!" gasped Mummy Bear.

Then Daddy Bear noticed his chair.
It wasn't how he'd left it.

"*Someone's* been
sitting in *my* chair!"
he roared.

"Oh my goodness!" gasped Mummy Bear.
"*Someone's* been sitting in *my* chair!"

"Mum!" screamed Baby Bear. "LOOK!"

"Someone's been sitting in my chair and they've broken it all up!"

"That someone is a *hooligan* and a *thief*," growled Daddy Bear, "and if I find them, there's going to be trouble!" Daddy Bear marched up the stairs. Mummy Bear and Baby Bear tiptoed up behind him.

Upstairs, things were just as bad.

"*Someone's* been sleeping
in *my* bed!" roared
Daddy Bear.

"Someone's been sleeping in *my* bed!" gasped Mummy Bear.

Baby Bear ran to
his room.
"Someone's been
sleeping in my bed,"
screamed Baby Bear,
"and she's still in it!"

"I don't believe it!"
growled Daddy Bear.
"It can't be true!"
gasped Mummy Bear.
But before anyone could
say another word,
Goldilocks leapt out of
bed. She was so frightened
her hair stood on end.

"Help! Help! Save me!" she
screamed and raced away.

The three bears laughed and laughed and laughed. "I'll never know how a little girl like that could be so naughty!" said Mummy Bear.

Goldilocks ran all the way home where she hid under her bed and didn't come out for a week. And she never poked her nose in other people's houses again.

OTHER BOOKS ILLUSTRATED BY EMMA CHICHESTER CLARK

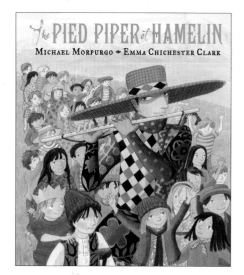

ISBN 978-1-4063-1511-0

ISBN 978-1-4063-2620-8

ISBN 978-1-4063-2288-0

ISBN 978-1-4063-2556-0

Available from all good bookshops

www.walker.co.uk